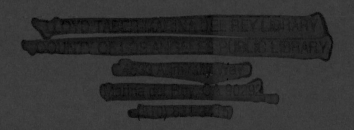

For Mom, who never tucked me in
without a story or two.
—A.M.

For Lily, with love.
—J.R.

Betsy B. Little

Text copyright © 2009 by Anne McEvoy

Illustrations copyright © 2009 by Jacqueline Rogers

Manufactured in China.

Library of Congress Cataloging-in-Publication Data is available.
ISBN 978-0-06-059337-7 (trade bdg.) — ISBN 978-0-06-059338-4 (lib. bdg.)

Design by Stephanie Bart-Horvath
1 2 3 4 5 6 7 8 9 10
❖
First Edition

Betsy B. Little
Was not small at all.
In fact, she was over
Eleven feet tall.

Wherever she went
She created a stir.
Why, even her dad
Had to look up at her.

The roof of her house

Was the highest in town.

When she looked at the treetops,

She had to look down.

She'd walk down the street
And she'd stop all the traffic,

And on family trips
She was unphotographic.

And skating for Betsy

Was truly a test.

Her four legs would go

North, south, east, and west!

A ride on the bus
Left her feeling a wreck,
And telephone wires
Were a pain in the neck!

Her schoolmates complained
When they couldn't see past her,

And jump rope was always
A total disaster.

At night, it was either
Her feet or her head
That had to hang over
One end of her bed.

But under her covers,
She'd smile away,
For night after night
Betsy dreamed of ballet. . . .

Where costumes and music,

The lights and the crowd

Made Betsy B. Little

Feel pretty and proud.

When she told her parents
She wanted to dance,
They said to each other,
"Let's give her a chance."

And so,

On the very first Monday in May,

She arrived

At the Skoffington School of Ballet.

She joined a class full
Of hopeful performers
In tutus and toe shoes
And tights and leg warmers.

She bowed and she curtsied
To old Miss Triano,
Who played them a waltz
On her purple piano.

It felt just like flying

On butterfly wings,

Graceful and lovely,

Except for two things. . . .

When Betsy B. leaped,
Her head hit the ceiling.
She landed so hard
It sent everyone reeling.

Her classmates all scattered
And started to squawk,
"With those legs and that neck,
Just be glad you can walk!"

The mothers all muttered,
"She's simply too tall.
The great ballerinas
Have always been small."

And when they all mumbled

And grumbled and such,

It made Betsy feel

Like not dancing so much.

The next week
Miss Skoffington whispered, "Dear me!
Someone is missing,
And it's Betsy B.!"

"Perhaps," said the others,
Who hoped it was true,
"She's found a more sensible
Dream to pursue."

"She's probably shopping
Or writing a letter
Or knitting a really long
Turtleneck sweater."

Now Betsy loved shopping

And was quite the knitter,

But Betsy B. Little

Was NEVER a quitter.

In fact, at this moment

She stood in the park.

The playground was empty,

The sky getting dark.

But she said, "Now or never!"
Her spirits were high.
No ceiling above her
Except for the sky.

One, two, three . . . two, two, three,

Into the air

Higher and higher

With headroom to spare!

From her very first jump
To her last pirouette,
Betsy thought,
"This is my best ballet yet."

"Maybe my problem's not
Being too tall.
Maybe I've simply been
Dreaming too small!"